A Grand Day

Words by
Jean Reidy

Pictures by
Samantha Cotterill

A Paula Wiseman Book • Simon & Schuster Books for Young Readers
New York • London • Toronto • Sydney • New Delhi

Backpack.
Pillow.
Blanket.
Bear.

Ring the doorbell.
Hide.
"Who's there?"

A million kisses!
Hugs! Hooray!

Our grand day
begins this way.

Jelly toast
with milk
and tea,
on the porch for
you and me.

Early birds eat
breakfast too!
Make a plan.
We've lots to do!

Plant
and pick
and pluck
and prune.
Dewy garden warms up soon.
Blue above and green below . . .

on grand days
all things
stretch and grow.

Paint and crayons
and clay or—
CHALK!—
down the driveway,
up the walk.

Dinos, rainbows,
names appear.

Masterpieces
made right here!

Grab the mitts.
I'll grab the spoon.
Mixing. Baking.
Nibbling soon.
Pack a basket.
Fill a plate.

Grand day goodies!
We can't wait!

Pull a wagon.
Choose our books.
Scout some shade.
Stake out our nooks.
Back-to-back or
side-by-side . . .

imaginations open wide.

Spread a picnic.
Sail our fleet.
Chat with furry friends
we meet.
Cool off toes,
then shins,
then knees.
Salute the sun.
Soak in the breeze.

Headstand! Cartwheel!
Cheering! Clapping!

(Grand days
need some time
for napping.)

Search and spy and snoop—
EXPLORE!—
on a shelf,
behind a door.

Grand old treasures
to uncover.
Grand new wonders
to discover.

Surprises!
Stories! In a box!
Dress-ups!
Dancing in our socks!

Try a two-step, maybe ten.
All that's old . . . is new again.

Set a table.
Mark each place.

Love and cheer
fill one snug space.
All the feasting,
all the fuss—

grand days include
ALL of us.

Night watch. Star wish.
Crickets call.
One mapped hand holds one so small.

Eyes so bright and smiles aglow.
Laughs like someone else we know.
Family ties so strong and true.

Part of me
is part of you.

Pile on blankets.
Night-lights dim.
Extra friends to cuddle in.

Tell a tale or three or more.
Whisper prayers we've heard before.
A well-loved song will pave the way
to dreams about . . .

our next Grand Day!

SIMON & SCHUSTER BOOKS FOR YOUNG READERS
An imprint of Simon & Schuster Children's Publishing Division
1230 Avenue of the Americas, New York, New York 10020
Text © 2022 by Jean Reidy
Illustration © 2022 by Samantha Cotterill
Book design by Lizzy Bromley © 2022 by Simon & Schuster, Inc.
All rights reserved, including the right of reproduction in whole or in part in any form.
SIMON & SCHUSTER BOOKS FOR YOUNG READERS
and related marks are trademarks of Simon & Schuster, Inc.
For information about special discounts for bulk purchases, please contact
Simon & Schuster Special Sales at 1-866-506-1949 or business@simonandschuster.com.
The Simon & Schuster Speakers Bureau can bring authors to your live event.
For more information or to book an event, contact the Simon & Schuster Speakers Bureau
at 1-866-248-3049 or visit our website at www.simonspeakers.com.
The text for this book was set in Altra Mano.
The illustrations for this book are hand built, mixed-media three-
dimensional sets photographed with a DSLR camera.
Manufactured in China
0322 SCP
First Edition
2 4 6 8 10 9 7 5 3 1
Library of Congress Cataloging-in-Publication Data
Names: Reidy, Jean, author. | Cotterill, Samantha, illustrator.
Title: A grand day / Jean Reidy ; illustrated by Samantha Cotterill.
Description: First edition. | New York : Simon & Schuster Books for Young
Readers, [2022] | "A Paula Wiseman Book." | Audience: Ages 4-8. | Audience: Grades 2-3. | Summary:
"Celebrates the special bond between grandparents and their grandchildren"—Provided by publisher.
Identifiers: LCCN 2021022258 | ISBN 9781534499768 (hardcover) | ISBN
9781534499751 (ebook)
Subjects: LCSH: Grandparent and child—Juvenile fiction. |
Grandparents—Juvenile fiction. | CYAC: Stories in rhyme. | Grandparent
and child—Fiction. | Grandparents—Fiction. | LCGFT: Stories in rhyme.
| Picture books.
Classification: LCC PZ8.3.R2676 Gr 2022 | DDC [E]—dc23
LC record available at https://lccn.loc.gov/2021022258

In memory of Fortunata Menoni

—J. R.

For all the grandparents
out there who hold our
hearts forever

—S. C.